Carl Reiner

Tell Me a SILLY STORY

ILLUSTRATED BY
JAMES BENNETT

Pickwick
Press

Once again,
thank you,
Nick Reiner.

ISBN-13: 978-1-60747-713-6
Library of Congress Cataloging-In-Publication Data Available

Illustration by James Bennett
Book Layout Design by Sonia Fiore

Printed in the United States of America
March 2010
1 0 5 2 0 1 0

Pickwick Press, an imprint of
Phoenix Books, Inc.
9465 Wilshire Boulevard, Suite 840
Beverly Hills, CA 90212

10 9 8 7 6 5 4 3 2 1

My grandpa always told me scary stories, and
I liked them a lot, but the last one he told me scared me
so much that I could not sleep for a whole week.

One night after dinner, I asked my
grandpa if he knew any silly stories.

Grandpa said, "I know a lot of silly stories.
How many do you want to hear?"

I shouted,
"This many,
Grandpa!"

"Okay, let's start with this one," Grandpa said.

"It's about a silly family I knew, whose last name was Sillie. Willie Sillie and his wife, Millie Sillie, and their children, Billy and Lilly."

On a chilly morning, the Sillie family moved into a house on a hilly street in the town of Philly-delphia.

Lilly Sillie made everyone laugh when she shouted shrilly,

"I am Lilly Sillie, and my brother Billy is chilly and would love a cup of hot chili!"

And that's how the Sillies met their new neighbors, Mr. and Mrs. Sutter Cutter and their twins, Hutter and Dutter. The Cutters lived in a house with many shutters and rooms full of clutter.

Hutter and Dutter loved to putter in the clutter.
Billy and Lilly thought it was great fun to putter in the clutter
with Hutter and Dutter while their parents had tea.

One day while eating lunch, Hutter's sister, Dutter, who like
Hutter also stuttered, was buttering her bread and muttering
about stuttering, when she saw a moth flutter
from the rain gutter, land on her butter,
then flutter from her butter back to the
gutter above her window shutter.

Dutter shouted excitedly,
"I just saw a moth flutter from the gutter to my butter,
then flutter back to the gutter above my shutter!"

And Dutter Cutter said it all without a stutter!

Miraculously, by uttering these words
without stuttering, Dutter had cured her stutter.

Billy, Lilly, and Dutter ran to Hutter and
told him how he too could cure his stutter.

It took many moths, many pats of butter, and many utter failures, but on the hundredth try, Hutter succeeded.

"Bless you, Mr. Moth," Hutter Cutter shouted. "I saw you flutter from the gutter to my butter, then flutter from my butter back to the gutter above my shutter!"

Hutter patted the moth on his fuzzy head and whispered, "Thank you! Your fluttering cured my stuttering!"

Then Grandpa told me another of his silly stories,
which he called the "Ish Story."
It was about Billy and Lilly Sillie's cousin Misha Stish.

Misha spoke English and Spanish and
loved to add "ish" to all words.

If you asked Misha Stish what he would like for
dinner and at what time, Misha would say,
"Eight-ish is okay-ish, nine-ish is fine-ish,
but ten-ish is too late-ish. And if it is all
right-ish with you, I prefer something fish-ish
rather than meat-ish or chicken-ish!"

When Misha Stish described his children, he would say,
"My son Stash Stish is twelve-ish and can wish
you a 'Happy Birthday' in English,
Spanish, Flemish, and Yiddish.

My daughter Trish is twenty-two-ish,
cute-ish, coquette-ish, peevish and is engaged
to a nebbish named Frobisch."

Grandpa said, "I am going to tell you one more silly story, and it is one of my favorites. It starts with the poem 'A Tutor Who Tutored the Flute' that was written by Billy and Lilly's uncle, Colonel Newt de Grute. That's a photo of him on the wall."

And Grandpa recited Colonel Newt de Grute's poem:

"A tutor who tutored the flute,
Tried to tutor two tooters to toot,
Said the two to the tutor,
Is it harder to toot,
Or tutor two tooters to toot?"

Colonel Newt de Grute was a lovable old coot
who not only taught two tooters to toot a flute, but taught
two tailors to tailor a suit, two cobblers to cobble a boot,
and two soldiers to aim and to shoot.

Colonel de Grute was a happy galoot, but he
could turn into a brute and bop a soldier on the snoot,
if the soldier walked by and failed to salute.

In nineteen fifty-two, Colonel Newt de Grute retired and bought a broad-shouldered, beaut of a suit—a "zoot suit."

Newt thought he looked dapper in his suit, but poor Newt was hooted for wearing a suit that was zooted.

The Sillies made fun of Newt's baggy
suit, but a flutist named Ruth, whom
Newt had once tutored to toot, found
Newt de Grute awfully cute and wisely
kept mute about his zooted suit.

Two months later, after
cleaning his fireplace,
Newt de Grute,
all covered with soot,
asked Ruth Levoot to
become Mrs. de Grute.

The de Grutes moved to Butte…
Montana, that is…with all their
loot and named their first-born
Hoot—after the old cowboy star,
Hoot Gibson.

I was sleepy, but I asked Grandpa to
tell me just one more silly story.

Grandpa told me one about a boy who fell asleep
laughing in the middle of the silliest story he ever told.

The next morning, I told Grandpa that
I dreamed that I was smiling and asked him,

"Did you see me smile?"

And he said,

"No, but I heard you laughing.
You kept me awake all night!"

I really like silly stories at bedtime—
I'll bet you do too! And the sillier the better!